Meet The Author - Jeremy Strong

What is your favourite animal?
A cat
What is your favourite boy's name?
Magnus Pinchbottom
What is your favourite girl's name?
Wobbly Wendy
What is your favourite food?
Chicken Kiev (I love garlic)
What is your favourite music?
Soft
What is your favourite hobby?
Sleeping

Meet The Illustrator - Scoular Anderson

What is your favourite animal?
Humorous dogs
What is your favourite boy's name?
Orlando
What is your favourite girl's name?
Esmerelda
What is your favourite food?
Garlicky, tomatoey pasta
What is your favourite music?
Big orchestras
What is your favourite hobby?
Long walks

Living with Vampires

by
Jeremy Strong

Illustrated by Scoular Anderson

First published in 2003 in Great Britain by
Barrington Stoke Ltd
18 Walker Street, Edinburgh, EH3 7LP
www.barringtonstoke.co.uk

This edition first published in 2009

Reprinted 2011

4u2read edition based on *Living With Vampires*, published by
Barrington Stoke in 2000

ISBN: 978-1-84299-796-3

Printed in Great Britain by Bell & Bain Ltd

Contents

Chapter 1
No Escape!

Kevin Vladd was not looking forward to Tuesday evening.

His parents, Mr and Mrs Vladd, were not looking forward to Tuesday evening.

And his teacher, Mrs Fottle, was not looking forward to Tuesday evening.

Tuesday was the day of the Parent-Teacher Meetings. 400 parents would meet up at the school with eight teachers. There was no escape.

Kevin did not like these meetings. He got on well with his teacher, Mrs Fottle. But he never knew what she was going to say next to his parents.

He did *try* to work at school. It was just that he had better things to do. He could sit and stare out of the window for hours looking at the clouds.

And if there weren't any clouds to gaze at, he could always stare at Miranda.

Miranda had long, black hair. Miranda had lovely, dark eyes. Miranda looked like a princess.

Kevin thought Miranda was Heaven on Legs.

The problem was that every other boy in the school thought Miranda was Heaven on Legs too. Grant more than anyone.

Kevin did not like Grant. But now that Tuesday had come, Kevin had other things to think about.

Kevin and his parents were waiting outside the classroom for Mrs Fottle to finish talking to Grant and his mum. *What will Mrs Fottle say about me*, Kevin thought. He hoped it would be something nice.

Kevin liked Mrs Fottle. Most of the time she was kind and helpful and said nice things about him. *Most* of the time.

Kevin's mum and dad hadn't met Mrs Fottle before. He hoped that it would all go well. He knew his parents had not had any supper before they came out. Kevin did not like to think what they might

do if they were hungry. But there was nothing he could do about it.

The classroom door opened and Grant and his mum came out. Grant stuck out his tongue. Kevin looked away. He went into the classroom with his parents.

"Kevin's maths has got better," Mrs Fottle began, "but I have to tell you that I think he has a problem."

Kevin sat up. What *had* he done? Had Mrs Fottle seen him flicking paper balls at Grant? Or staring at Miranda in class?

Kevin's dad got a little closer to Mrs Fottle. A bit too close, Kevin thought.

"What's this problem?" he asked.

Mrs Fottle opened a folder of work. "I asked everyone to draw a picture of their dad or mum," she said. "And Kevin drew this. There's an awful lot of blood in it, don't you think?"

She held up the picture and Kevin's parents looked at it. He had drawn his father with Dracula fangs. Blood was dripping from them.

Kevin's mum clapped her hands and smiled at her husband. "Darling, it looks just like you!"

Mrs Fottle did not think it was funny. She began to huff and puff. "This is not a joke. This drawing is *very* upsetting. And Kevin has handed in other pictures like this one."

Mrs Fottle pulled out some more sheets of paper. "Look at this one – zombies! And this one – vampires! I really think Kevin should see someone. All that blood. There must be awful things going on in his head."

Kevin's dad smiled. "The thing is, Mrs Fottle, it's not in his head." He lifted back his upper lip and showed her his teeth.

Mrs Fottle took one look at the sharp, white fangs and went very pale. "Oh," she said, softly. "Oh, dear. I think I'm going to faint."

And she did. She fell forwards across her desk.

Kevin's mum clapped her hands. "Supper!" she cried. "I'm starving."

Kevin's parents sank their teeth into Mrs Fottle's neck.

Kevin's parents were Grade Three vampires. No wonder he was in a state.

Chapter 2

All You Need To Know About Vampires

There are four kinds of vampires.

Grade One are the most scary. They only come out at night. They lie in their coffins all day. These are the ones you often see in films or read about in books. They have white faces and fangs that drip blood. They can turn into bats and fly about. They suck blood and leave lots of bodies around, which is very untidy.

Grade Two vampires have less power. They can also turn into bats. They leave lots of dead bodies around too. It's not very nice if you step on one.

Like the Grade Ones, Grade Two vamps only come out at night, but they don't have coffins. They just lie about all day in damp, dark caves, getting wet and muddy.

Grade Three vampires can go out in daylight. They suck people's blood, but they can't kill anyone. Their victims just faint and when they wake up they can't remember what it was all about.

Grade Three vampires can turn people into zombies, but even that wears off after a while. They live in houses and sleep in beds, which is very sensible of them.

Grade Four vampires are hopeless. They can't even suck blood. They just lick your skin, which is revolting. All the other vampires agree that Grade Fours are A Big Joke.

But, if *your* parents are vampires, it's no joke at all. Even if they're only Grade Three.

Kevin was unlucky in another way. He was the only non-vampire in his family. Every 100 years a vampire family has *one* child who is *not* a vampire. Kevin was that child.

What Kevin wanted more than anything was to have normal parents. He wanted to be able to go out with them and know they would not sink their fangs into someone's neck.

Most of all he wanted to go to the School Disco. He wanted to dance with Miranda, the most beautiful girl in the school.

The problem was that the disco was for staff, children *and* their parents. If Kevin went to the disco, his parents would have to go too.

Kevin's parents liked discos. But he hadn't even told them about this one yet. How could he take a pair of vampires to a disco? Anything could happen. Kevin gave a sigh.

How can I tell Mum and Dad not to come?

His parents had finished their meal and were wiping the blood from their fangs with some paper tissues.

Mrs Vladd smiled at her son. "Mrs Fottle said that your maths is much better."

"Mum, I don't care about my maths," said Kevin. "Will Mrs Fottle be OK?"

"Oh, she'll be OK. When she wakes up she won't remember a thing. Now, what's all this about a School Disco?"

Kevin's mum had seen the big poster on the classroom wall. "You haven't said a thing about it. I thought you liked discos. Are we all going?"

Kevin gave another sigh. His parents often made him sigh.

Chapter 3
How To Cure A Vampire

After the Parent-Teacher meeting,
Mrs Fottle had to take three days off work.
She said she felt worn out. She didn't
remember what had happened. But it was
all too much for Kevin.

Things couldn't go on like this. The
shame was too much for him. And it was
scary.

The School Disco was coming up. He wanted to go so much. But if he went, his parents would go too. Miranda would be there. How could he put her in such danger?

Kevin knew that somehow he would have to stop his parents being vampires. He had five days to find out how to do it.

He sat in his bedroom and thought and thought. And then it came to him.

GARLIC!

Vampires hate garlic. If he could get his parents to eat a lot of garlic, it would stop them being vampires.

Kevin found just the right dish for them. Chicken stuffed with garlic butter.

It was quite a shock for Kevin's mum when he told her he wanted to cook them all a meal. "You can't even make toast," she said.

"You just wait and see," Kevin said. "And keep out of the kitchen."

Kevin got to work. He wanted the meal to stop his parents from being vampires for the rest of their lives, so he put in an awful lot of garlic. He was thrilled! He was sure this was going to work.

Kevin laid the table and called for his parents.

"It does smell nice," said Dad. "What is it?"

"Try it and see," said Kevin. Kevin's mum and dad stuffed some chicken into their mouths. Dad began to choke. He fell off his chair. His whole plate of chicken was sent zooming out of the window.

At the same time Kevin's mum went mad. Her eyes grew as big as plates. She jumped up from her chair and began to hop from one foot to the other.

Then she rushed to the bathroom and threw herself under the shower with all her clothes on. She stood there with her mouth open, gulping down cold water.

Kevin grabbed a jug of water and tipped it down Dad's throat.

Kevin's parents spent the next day in bed. He was banned from cooking anything ever again.

Kevin didn't mind about being banned from the kitchen. But his problem had not gone away. How could he stop his parents from being vampires in time for the School Disco?

And if he didn't go to the School Disco he knew who would dance with Miranda. Grant, of course.

Chapter 4
Big Feet, Big Trouble

Grant was very tall and very good-looking. He was also very full of himself and a bit of a bully.

Kevin hated Grant.

Grant hated Kevin.

Kevin kept well away from Grant because he had long arms, with fists, and long legs, with boots.

For some odd reason, Miranda seemed to like Grant. Kevin didn't know why. It made him very upset.

And what was he going to do about his parents who were still vampires?

Kevin went to the School Library to see what he could find out about vampires.

But there was only one book about vampires and that was full of stupid jokes.

What is a vampire's best word?

Fang-tastic!

Then Miranda came into the library. Kevin almost fell off his chair. He looked around. He was alone with Miranda! At last he could ask her to dance with him at the School Disco!

Miranda saw Kevin and came over to him. She stood so close that Kevin could hear her breathing.

She just looked at him. She didn't smile. She never, never smiled. He would love to make her smile. He stared up at her.

"Why are you reading a book about vampires?" she asked.

"I don't know. It was just lying here."

Miranda nodded.

There was a long silence.

I must stop staring at her, Kevin thought.

Kevin looked at Miranda's feet. She was wearing a pair of dinky, pink trainers.

What could he say? He must say *something*. "What size shoes do you wear?" he asked her. And as he said this, he thought, *Kevin, you are the biggest dumbo in dumbo-land.*

Miranda hit him with the vampire book.

BLIPP!

"Are you saying I've got big feet? You are *so* rude!"

BLAPP!

Miranda hit him again and rushed out of the library.

Kevin just sat there. How could he have been so stupid? Why hadn't he asked her to dance with him at the disco? Why did he ask her about shoe sizes?

He was just putting the vampire book back when he saw another book lying on the shelf.

ALL ABOUT HYPNOSIS.

Chapter 5
Look Into My Eyes ...

Kevin started to read the book on hypnosis. He began to get more and more excited. The book said that hypnosis could be used to stop people smoking, or snoring, or eating too much. You could use hypnosis to make people do what you wanted.

Kevin could use hypnosis to stop his parents being vampires. All he had to do was to put them into a dream state.

Kevin would need to swing something from side to side in front of his parents. They would stare at it and would slowly slip into this dream state. Then he could tell them to do just what he wanted. Great!

As soon as he got home that afternoon, Kevin got out his yo-yo and tried it out in front of the mirror. He swung it from side to side. He stared at it. He spoke softly to himself.

"You are feeling sleepy ... you are feeling sleepy ..."

BANG!

He fell asleep and crashed to the floor. It had worked! All he had to do now was to try the same trick on his parents and hypnotise them.

His mum and dad were in the front room, watching TV. Kevin went in and smiled at them. "Can I show you a trick with my yo-yo?" he said.

"Will it take long?" said his mum. She wanted to get back to the TV.

"No. It's very quick," Kevin told her.

Kevin sat his parents close to each other and swung the yo-yo from side to side in front of them. "Keep looking at it," he began in a soft voice. The yo-yo went from side to side. Mum's and Dad's eyes went from side to side too. Their heads began to nod.

"You're feeling sleepy," Kevin said. "You can't keep your eyes open. You are asleep … asleep … in a deep sleep."

Mum began to snore. Soon they were both propping each other up, fast asleep.

Kevin went on. "You will never want to suck blood again. You will stop being vampires. You will be nice, normal people."

He stopped and looked at his parents. They were still asleep and snoring. Things were looking good.

"Raise your right arm," said Kevin. They both slowly raised their right arms. His parents were in his power! He could make them do – ANYTHING!

"Dad, stick your finger in Mum's ear. Mum, stick your finger up Dad's nose."

Kevin was laughing so much he couldn't go on. But now he knew that the hypnosis was working.

"I will count up to three and you will both wake up. You will not remember anything. One, two, three!"

"What's been going on?" asked his dad as he woke up.

"I was showing you a trick with my yo-yo," Kevin said and smiled.

And that was that. All Kevin could do now was to sit back and wait and see. Were his parents cured of being vampires at last?

Chapter 6
The Letter

Three days went by. Kevin's parents didn't bite anyone. It was great. He no longer had to live with vampire parents!

He could safely go to the School Disco and so could everyone else. All he had to do now was to see if he could get Miranda to dance with him. Maybe she would if he said he was sorry he'd asked about her shoe size.

There was only one day to go, so Kevin didn't have much time. The problem was that Miranda always had a huge crowd of boys around her. Grant was always there. Kevin could never see her alone.

Kevin made up his mind that he would write her a letter. He worked on it in the maths lesson. He had to get it just right.

"Kevin? Kevin? Are you with us Kevin? Is there anyone in? Kevin?"

It was Mrs Fottle. She was standing next to him, gazing down.

She shook her head. "You were miles away. I was going to ask if you could tell us what a triangle is called if it's three sides are the same length. But I can see that you are doing something far more important. Let's see what you've been writing. No,

don't try to hide it. I want to have a look.
Thank you."

Mrs Fottle picked up the letter. She began
to read it out loud. "*I didn't mean to say
that you have got big feet.*"

The rest of the class began to laugh.

Mrs Fottle read on. "*I think you have the most beautiful feet in the world.*"

The class exploded. Some kids were clutching their sides they were laughing so much. "*I would die to have feet like yours.*"

Now half the class were rolling about on the floor.

Mrs Fottle put the note back on Kevin's desk. "Well," she began, "I wonder who this note is for? Would you like to tell us?"

Kevin wanted to die. How could he tell everyone in the class that it was for Miranda? She was staring hard at him. Kevin knew that if he said the letter was for her she would never, never speak to him again.

Kevin looked up at his teacher. "It's for you, Mrs Fottle."

Everyone stopped laughing and stared at Kevin with their mouths open.

Mrs Fottle knew the letter wasn't for her. But what she did next was something that Kevin would always remember.

"It's a private letter," she said. "I'm very sorry, Kevin, I should never have read it out at all."

And she meant it. The class stopped laughing. Mrs Fottle went back to her desk and sat down. She began to talk about maths again.

Kevin couldn't write his letter after that. And he would never be able to speak to Miranda now. His whole life was a mess.

As soon as he got home, Kevin went up to his room and threw himself on his bed. He had made his parents stop being vampires, but the one thing he wanted most would never happen now.

However, when Kevin opened up his school bag he found a note.

Dear Kevin,

Those were such sweet things to say about my feet. I would like to dance with you at the disco. See you there!

Love, Miranda xxx

Kevin read the letter at least 50 times.

Chapter 7
The School Disco

When Kevin walked into the school hall on disco night, he knew he was going to remember it always. His mum and dad hadn't done anything a vampire would do for over a week now. Kevin was sure that the hypnosis had worked. They would never suck blood again.

The hall looked fantastic. The disco was in full swing. Music was pounding. Kevin looked around in the dim light for Miranda.

"Come and dance!" someone said behind him.

Kevin swung round. It was Mum. She grabbed him and began to twist and turn. Kevin could have died with shame. He prayed that Miranda wouldn't see him dancing with his own mum.

Then he saw Miranda, just for a moment. She was sitting on the far side of the hall. She looked like an angel, but an angel with a frown. Once again Kevin longed to make her smile.

There were boys all around her, but she wasn't going to dance. Grant was standing beside her, but she wasn't even looking at him.

Kevin smiled. He had Miranda's note in his pocket. He knew Miranda was waiting just for him. Soon he would be dancing with her. He began to make his way across the hall.

"Kevin! Come and dance. Tell me you've forgiven me." This time it was Mrs Fottle.

This disco was like a very bad dream! First of all his mum and now his teacher!

"I can't dance with you," began Kevin, but Mrs Fottle held him to her chest and spun him round until he was dizzy.

"You're a great dancer," she said.

"I've got to go now," Kevin said. "Thank you for the dance."

He rushed off. Where was Miranda? She had gone and the boys around her had gone too. Kevin's heart began to pound. He mustn't lose her now!

And that was when the screaming began.

Scared boys and girls were rushing around yelling. Parents and teachers hung on to each other for safety.

But why?

And then Kevin saw the first zombie. It was Grant. He was coming through the hall with his arms held out in front of him. His face was white and his eyes had rolled up inside his head. He looked revolting.

Kevin looked at Grant's neck. Yes! He could see two fang-holes. Kevin's heart sank into his boots. The hypnosis had worn off. His parents had gone back to being vampires.

Behind Grant was another zombie and another and another! Now there were

zombies everywhere. They were stomping through the hall and all around them people yelled and waved their arms about and fainted in great big heaps.

Behind the zombies Kevin could see his parents. They hadn't had any fresh blood for two weeks and now they had a whole heap of people to choose from. This was the disaster he had been trying to stop all along.

Then Kevin had an awful thought. Miranda! She was in danger! She was standing, still frowning, right next to his parents. He must save her!

Kevin dashed across the hall. He pushed the zombies aside.

He rushed past his parents and grabbed Miranda. "This way!" he shouted. "I'll save you! I'll get you out of here! Come on!"

Kevin and Miranda ran to the hall door. "Don't let go of my hand! Come on, this way. We'll be safe down here!"

They ran down a dark passage. Kevin threw open the library door.

At last they stopped panting. Miranda was standing right next to Kevin. He could almost hear her heart beat.

She was still gripping his hand.

Kevin wanted this moment to last for ever. He was alone at last with Miranda! She gazed at him.

"You are *so* brave, Kevin," she said. He turned and looked at her and at last she smiled at him.

And that was when Kevin saw that it was not his parents who had caused the disaster at the disco.

Miranda had fangs. *She* was the vampire.

And he had left his yo-yo at home.

Problems with a Python

by
Jeremy Strong

Adam's got a problem and it's out of control!
A snake has escaped. It's loose in the school
and it's Adam's fault! Can he find it before
things get wildly out of hand?

You can order *Problems with a Python 4u2read edition* from
our website at www.barringtonstoke.co.uk

Ghost for Sale

by
Terry Deary

Who would like to see a ghost?
Mr Rundle spots in the paper that there is a
ghost for sale inside a wardrobe. Should he
buy it? He needs something to make people
come to his inn. But will people want to sleep
in a room with a ghost?

You can order *Ghost for Sale 4u2read edition* from our
website at www.barringtonstoke.co.uk